too hot to handle

EMMA BRAY

one

Jay

"HOW DID you let this happen, man?"

"I don't know," Doug answers, his voice anguished. "I swear it was a mistake, Jay. I borrowed the money from the company to tide me over until my next paycheck. I was going to put it back. I swear to God. You've got to believe me, man."

It doesn't matter what I believe. I don't tell Doug that, though. Doug is my roommate from college. He was always a bit wild and irresponsible. Apparently, having a child hasn't changed him. Same old Doug.

I don't ask him how much he "borrowed" and forgot to put back. None of my business.

But why did he use me for his one phone call?

He gets to the point soon enough. "Will you watch my little girl for me while I'm in here?"

I pause.

"They're taking the house," he says into the silence. "My baby girl won't have anywhere to go."

"You don't have anyone else, man?" I ask him cautiously. I don't mind helping him out, but Jesus, I haven't seen his daughter since she was eight years old. What if she's not comfortable with me?

"My parents are both dead, and my dead wife's parents want nothing to do with us. Layla has never even met them, and you know I don't have any siblings, so there's no one else."

My mind is spinning. I'm a certified bachelor. I know next to nothing about taking care of kids.

When I remain silent, still trying to wrap my head around everything, Doug adds with a note of desperation to his voice, "Please, Jay. Make sure nothing happens to my girl. I don't care about anything else. I don't care about losing the house. I don't care how long they lock me up. I need to know she's safe. And I can't think of anyone I would entrust her to more than you."

Doug may have fucked up, but his concern for his daughter is genuine, and what kind of friend would I be if I didn't help him?

"Of course, man. You know I'll do it."

Doug and I aren't as close as we were in college, but he's still an old buddy, and I can't in good conscience leave his daughter to fend for herself because of her father's fuck up.

Relief floods Doug's voice. "Thanks, man. You're doing me a solid. You have no idea how much this eases my mind."

"You got it. Focus on getting your shit together, and don't worry about Layla. I'll take care of her."

My first glimpse of Layla almost knocks me over. I don't know what I expected. Doug told me his daughter is now a senior in high school, so I knew she was eighteen, but nothing could have prepared me for the perfect blonde angel standing before me.

The last time I saw Layla, she was eight years old with big blue eyes and pigtails. She's still got the big blue eyes, but now they're framed by thick, dark lashes, and her blonde hair flows down her back to the top of a perfectly rounded ass. My mouth goes dry, and my cock rises in my jeans at the sight of it. It's the kind of ass that turns men into animals.

"Uncle Jay!" she screams before she flings herself into my arms, wrapping her arms and legs around me.

And oh, sweet Jesus, her perfect little cunt, so soft and sweet, settles right against my nasty erection. It's hard for me to breathe. I suck in deep, gulping breaths, but it only fills my nose with her sweet berries scent. She smells young and ripe and oh so fucking innocent.

I gently unwind her arms from my neck and set her on the ground.

I'm confused at her exuberance to see me. "Do you remember me, sweetheart?"

She bobs her head up and down excitedly. "Of course! I was only a little girl, but I never forgot you, Uncle Jay!"

She giggles. Fucking *giggles*, and my god, the sound is more beautiful than a choir of angels singing.

I swallow at the worship shining in her innocent eyes, feeling like a complete scumbag for the hard-on tenting my pants for this sweet girl. Doesn't stop my eyes from sweeping over her tight, young body, though. She's got a pair of lush, ripe tits peeking out from the top of a form-fitting tank top, and those little booty shorts barely cover her sweet kitty.

I tear my eyes from her body, completely ashamed of myself. I'm sick. Here I am, thirty-five years old, and this girl is eighteen. I have no business reacting to her this way—not to mention she's my buddy's daughter, for Christ's sake. Which means I'm old enough to be her father.

"You remember me, Uncle Jay?" Her sweet voice cuts into my thoughts.

I drag my eyes back up to her innocent face. She has perfectly puffy pink lips made for sucking cock. She's the most innocent-looking angel princess I've ever seen.

All I can do is grunt. "You've grown up a lot since I last saw you."

She flips her hair and beams at me like I've given her the greatest compliment. "Yep! I'm not a little girl anymore," she pronounces proudly.

Fuck yes, you are, baby doll. You're Daddy's little girl.

I blink, mortified at my thoughts. Where the *fuck* did that come from?

"Are you ready?" I ask her, uncomfortable as hell with this entire situation. It never occurred to me that Doug's daughter would grow up to be a beautiful angel. Everything about her is light and perky and pretty. It almost hurts to look at her.

And *fuucck*, having her barely legal pussy parading

around my house in skimpy outfits like this is going to make however long Doug is locked up unbearable.

She peers up at me innocently. "Are you okay?"

"Yeah," I answer her gruffly. "Where's your stuff?" I'm studiously avoiding her tits and her perfect stomach, and hell, even her face. There's nowhere I can look that doesn't cause my cock to swell painfully in my jeans.

She tips her head to the side and regards me thoughtfully. "You've got this funny look like you're in pain or something."

I let out a humorless chuckle.

She frowns. "Are you?"

"Am I what?" I hedge.

She doesn't let it go. "In pain?" she asks me frankly, innocently.

"Fuck, yes," I croak. "But don't you worry about it. It's not your problem."

She bites her lip and looks at me with worry in those blue pools. "Is there anything I can do to help you?"

I laugh in shame. This sweet angel is worried about me being in pain. She has no idea that the only thing hurting is my filthy fucking cock, straining to bust through these jeans and get to her tight little pussy.

Fuck yeah, being buried balls deep in her little virgin pussy will help me.

And I know her pussy is untapped. It's written all over her—from those innocent blue eyes down to the hot pink nail polish on the tips of her toes.

I shake my head. *Focus. She's your friend's daughter. Stop thinking about her blue eyes and her pink toenails. And for the love of all things holy, make your dick go down.*

"Don't worry about me. Where's your stuff?"

My cock laughs at me and swells even harder in my jeans when Layla turns around and bends over to pick up one of her bags. Her sweet ass is pushed up in the air, and I ball my hands into fists to keep from grabbing her hips and humping against her like a wild animal.

The irony of the situation isn't lost on me. I've never reacted to a woman so strongly in my life, and the one time I do, she's a fucking teenager nearly half my age entrusted into my care by a good friend.

I take the bag from her and grab her other bags, nodding my head at the car. "Go get in the car, princess."

She pauses when I call her princess and looks up at me from beneath lowered lashes, her cheeks turning pink.

Fuck, if my cock wasn't already straining against my zipper, it sure as hell is now. She *likes* it when I call her princess. It's written all over her pretty little virgin face.

"Sure thing, Uncle Jay." She smiles up at me brightly before skipping over to my vehicle.

Moisture leaks from the tip of my cock, and I take a moment to turn away from her and readjust myself. I close my eyes and inhale deeply, trying to control my visceral response to her.

I begin to pray. *Lead me not into temptation...*

When I open my eyes again, Layla is bent over with her sweet ass in the air again.

Fuuuck.

two

Layla

"WHAT ARE YOU DOING?" Uncle Jay's voice barks at me.

I straighten and hold up the ring clutched between my fingers. "It was my mother's." I show it to him. "It's too big for me, so it keeps sliding off my finger, but I couldn't leave it behind."

He grunts by way of answer as he marches over to me and opens the passenger door of his SUV. He's standing so close to me, I can smell the spicy scent of his cologne.

My eyes travel up to his firm jaw. His big chest is

heaving up and down. "Are you sure you're okay, Uncle Jay?" I ask him again.

His nostrils flare, and he visibly swallows, but instead of answering, he tells me, "Get in the car, princess."

Princess. I instinctively clench my legs together. I don't know why that word from his lips affects me. All I know is it causes a pulsing at the apex of my thighs.

My legs are shaking as I step up into the SUV. Jay stands behind me the whole time. I can feel his eyes on me. When I'm seated, he leans into the vehicle, pulls the seatbelt over me, and clicks it into place. I stare at the stubble lining his jaw.

When he looks up, our eyes meet. His eyes are a beautiful stormy gray. They're unlike any color I've ever seen before. His minty breath fans across my lips, and my nipples pebble in my tank top. Good lord, Uncle Jay is so hot. Well, he's not *really* my uncle, but it's what I called him when I was a little girl.

I haven't seen him for years, but I know he and my father talked on the phone occasionally. I remember him being big and tall, but I never noticed just how gigantic he is. He straightens out of the vehicle, and I stare at him in awe, watching his muscles flex with each movement.

He throws my bags in the trunk before he walks

around to the driver's side and slides in. My eyes flick down to his thighs. They're built like cannons, big and meaty and just oh my god, the man is huge *everywhere*. This SUV is huge, yet he seems to take up the entire space. There's no way he'd fit in a sports vehicle. At barely five feet tall, I'm tiny in comparison and don't even reach his chest when standing. He's big enough to crush me with one hand. I don't know why the thought excites me, but it does.

My breathing quickens, and more moisture pools between my thighs. It suddenly occurs to me that maybe Uncle Jay is surly because he doesn't want me living with him.

My stomach drops at the thought. I don't want to be a burden. I'm eighteen, so technically, I'm an adult. I can live on my own. Yeah, I'm a senior in high school, but I can still go to school and find somewhere to live. Can't I? I chew on my lip.

"You know, you don't have to do this, Uncle Jay." I give him an out. "I'm eighteen, so I can live on my own."

His head whirls to look at me. "Absolutely fucking not!"

I should probably be offended at his authoritarian tone, but it causes liquid heat to pool deep inside me. I *like* it when he takes that tone with me, though I don't know why.

I clench my thighs tighter. Uncle Jay's eyes cut down to them before he shakes his head and curses under his breath, frowning deeper.

His behavior confuses me. "You seem to be mad at me or something."

His big chest heaves up and down again like he can't suck in enough air, and he sends me a look I can't decipher. "Not mad at you, princess. That's not it at all."

"Well, then, what is it, Uncle Jay?"

His hands grip the steering wheel so tightly that his knuckles turn white, and he grits, "Don't call me that."

My brow furrows. "What?"

"Uncle Jay." He speaks from behind clenched teeth. "I'm not your uncle, Layla."

I pause. Is that what has him so upset? "What do I call you then?"

"Call me Jay."

"Jay." I test out his name. It might be my imagination, but I think I see a shudder pass through his big frame.

And that fills me with a rush of feminine power.

"Does my presence bother you?" I ask him.

His jaw flexes as he glances over at me and says hoarsely. "It's not you. It's me."

"What do you mean?" My eyes widen when I see the bulge in his pants growing bigger. My heart rate ticks up as my breathing becomes hot and heavy.

When he doesn't answer my question, I ask, "Why can't I live on my own, Jay?"

He repeats firmly, "You can't live alone."

"Why not?" I press. I don't know why I'm pushing him, just that it feels *right* to do so.

He glances over at me and licks his lips before wiping his forehead with the back of his hand and flicking the air conditioning on high. "It's not safe for a pretty thing like you all alone. Men would beat down the door trying to get to you." He shakes his head. "Can't have that."

My face flushes with pleasure as I realize Jay called me pretty. I lean closer to him over the seat. "You think I'm pretty?"

He glances at me, sweat beading on his upper lip this time. "Pretty is an understatement. You're beautiful. Bet you drive all the boys crazy, don't you?" Jay's fingers flex on the steering wheel, and his shoulders are tense.

I shake my head. "Dad never let me date."

Jay seems to relax somewhat. "No fucking wonder.

He knew he'd have to beat them off you with a stick if he did."

I don't know what he's talking about, but the tone of his voice makes my stomach all fluttery. I realize something I haven't considered until this moment. "But I'm eighteen now, so I can date if I want to."

Jay's frown deepens, and his hands grip the steering wheel so hard I'm surprised he doesn't snap it in half.

"Over my dead body," he growls.

I frown at him, though a small part of me thrills at how he says it.

He glances over at me and adds, "Your father trusts me to take care of you, Layla. If he doesn't want you dating boys, we should abide by his rules."

"I don't have to date a boy," I tell him. "You can take me on my first date."

The car jerks and Jay nearly runs off the road before he regains control of the vehicle.

He gapes over at me before closing his mouth, his throat working. Suddenly, I know Jay is the only one I want to take me on my first date. In fact, I want him to be my first *everything*.

"Layla, I'm old enough to be your father," he finally says.

I shrug. "So what? Dad said I can't go on a date

with boys, so *you* take me on a date, Jay. You're not a boy. You're a man."

Jay sputters for a moment before he settles on, "Exactly."

But I'm completely married to this idea now. I want this big, hulking, sexy man to be the one to show me how a man treats a woman. I know Jay would take care of me the way a man is supposed to. A high school boy would never compare. "Jay, I'm eighteen, and I've never been on a date. Please?"

Jay looks at me, his jaw slack. "It would be inappropriate. Hell, Layla, you're going to be living with me. You're basically my ward."

"No, I'm not," I tell him stubbornly. "You're not my legal guardian."

"Layla," he says my name in that firm, authoritative tone, and my nipples start aching.

"You're my friend's daughter. You're going to be living with me, and I'm way too old for you. This subject is closed."

"But—"

He cuts me off with a stern look.

Muscles I didn't even know I had flutter. I bite my lip and look at him pleadingly.

His nostrils flare, and he holds my gaze for a beat before turning his eyes back to the road and pulling into a driveway. He slams the car into park with a curse and flings open the door, stomping out like an angry bull.

I hide the smile tugging at my lips. I don't know why I like seeing him so worked up like this, but I do, so I go with it.

And I'm sure this makes me a shitty daughter, but I'm glad I have to stay here with Jay. It's not like I'm happy my father is in jail, but he made his bed, and now he has to lie in it. He's notorious for making stupid financial decisions. The bank is repossessing the house, and there's nowhere else I want to live than with Jay.

three

Jay

I CANNOT BELIEVE my friend's beautiful eighteen-year-old daughter asked me to take her on a date. Fuck, I'd love to have her beautiful self on my arm, but it's wrong on so many levels.

I grit my teeth and will my dick to go down as she jumps out of the SUV like a little bunny rabbit. She hops up beside me and looks at me like I hang the fucking moon. I don't know what the hell I ever did to have this girl look at me so worshipfully, but it's going to make this a million times harder knowing she seems to want me too.

God hates me. That must be it. Why else would he send me this perfect girl as the ultimate temptation? Supple and young and completely off-limits.

I can only imagine what her father would say if he could see the bulge tenting my pants over his daughter. He'd take me out into the street and shoot me, and I would deserve it.

I'm a dirty fucking bastard.

"Come on, princess. Let's get you settled in."

I see how her eyes flutter when I call her "princess," and my cock swells so tight in my jeans it feels like it's going to bust through the zipper.

I should probably stop calling her that, but fuck if I can control it. It slips out whenever I'm around her. How can something so wrong feel so right?

I grab her bags and show her to the guest bedroom. Unfortunately, it doesn't have a bathroom, so she'll be sharing mine.

The thought of her naked body in my bathroom is enough to send a jet of precum shooting from the tip of my cock. I ball my hands into fists and bite back the groan threatening to rumble out of my chest.

Her eyes flick to my balled-up hands, and I make a conscious effort to release them.

"You seem so tense," she whispers.

"I'm fine," I deny, but hell no, I'm not fine. The

prettiest, sexiest girl I've ever met will be right down the hall from my bedroom all night, and it's going to take every ounce of self-control I have not to sneak in here like a thief and steal her little cherry.

"You know...I can rub you," she offers.

I nearly choke, and my throat closes up. "What?" I finally rasp.

She blinks at me innocently before she nods her head eagerly. "That's what I want to do when I graduate."

My vision goes red.

"I want to become a massage therapist."

Her voice cuts into the visuals in my head and calms me down. My shoulders relax as I realize what she's talking about. She's offering to give me a *massage*—not rub my dick.

God, the thought that she knows how to rub a dick almost blinded me with rage. I don't even want to think of her tiny hands on some boy's cock.

I inhale deeply and run a shaky hand through my hair. I know she's right. I'm wound up tighter than a spring, but the last thing I need is this angel's hands on me. If she puts those perfect little fingers on me, I'll combust.

So, I ignore her comment. "You need to go to bed soon. You've got school in the morning."

She pouts, and it's the most adorable thing I've ever seen. I swallow as I pull my eyes away from those puffy pink lips. "How do you usually get there?"

"I walk."

I frown, not liking her answer. "Not anymore, you don't. I'll drop you off."

She gives me a radiant smile which tells me she loves the idea. "Thank you, Jay."

My chest swells with pride, and I return her smile before finally coming back to my senses. I clear my throat. "If you need anything, I'm down the hall."

I force myself to leave her room, praying a bit of space will help this insane attraction.

I haven't been in my room for long, willing my dick to go down, when I hear the shower turn on. Images of her naked body flash through my mind, and it's all I can do not to rub one out while imagining the water sliding down her supple young flesh.

With a scowl, I strip down to my boxers and slide into bed, determined not to masturbate to thoughts of the innocent young girl down the hall in my home.

Those perky breasts.

That perfect ass.

Those innocent eyes.

That sinful mouth.

The way she asked me to take her on a date.

Fuuuck.

I remind myself I've got work in the morning, and Layla has school. If that contrast doesn't make my dick go down, nothing will.

Layla

Thunder booms again, and I jump. Call me a baby, but I've always hated storms. I hop out of bed with barely a thought and run down the hall to Jay's room. I don't even knock on the door before I go flying through it.

Jay sits up in bed, immediately alert, his big chest heaving up and down. "Layla, what's wrong?"

I finally skid to a stop at the side of his bed and shuffle my feet nervously. I bite my lip, feeling ridiculous. "It's storms," I whisper. "I hate them."

Jay's eyes soften, and he lets out a breath. His shoulders relax once he realizes there's no real danger. "It's okay, princess. The storm can't hurt you."

When I keep standing there uncertainly, Jay looks up at me, his eyes sweeping over me from head to toe. I blush when I realize I'm wearing nothing but a tiny tank top and a pair of panties. It's what I sleep in, and I didn't think twice about what I was wearing before I skittered over here like a frightened mouse.

Jay grips the covers in his hands as another flash of lightning illuminates the room, followed by a crack of thunder.

With a squeal, I slide beneath the covers with Jay. He immediately stiffens and pulls away from me like he's been burned. I'm so frightened that his withdrawal doesn't register enough to hurt my feelings.

"What are you doing?" His voice is raspy, and it makes my toes curl. Gosh, I love Jay's deep, masculine voice.

"Can I sleep here with you, Jay? Please?" I beg him, terrified to be alone.

"Fuck, Layla." Jay runs a hand over his face. "This isn't appropriate."

"Please? I'm scared." I'm not lying. Not only am I in a new place, but storms terrify me.

Jay frowns when he notes my trembling form. "God, Layla, look at you. You're trembling." He sighs and looks at me with soft, sympathetic eyes. "You're genuinely scared of storms?"

I nod again.

He sits in indecisive silence before letting out a long exhale and lying down.

My heart leaps in victory.

He keeps a careful distance between us as he says, "Yes, you can sleep in here, but only for tonight."

We lie there in awkward silence for a few moments until I finally whisper, "Jay?"

"Yeah." His voice is a strangled rasp.

"Will you hold me?"

He makes a tortured sound. "Fuck, Layla, I don't think that's a good—"

His words trail off whenever I scoot closer to him. I curl close to him and breathe deeply, allowing his comforting scent to wash over me. He's so big and warm, and I feel safe in his presence.

"Motherfuck," he grumbles under his breath before he finally opens his arms and allows me to settle in.

I happily snuggle into him, and oh my god, I feel so at home here. Everything about Jay is big and makes me feel safe—like nothing could ever hurt me again.

He strokes his hands through my hair, petting me like a kitten, as he asks gruffly, "Do you want to talk about it?"

I let out a stuttering breath. "There's nothing to talk about. I've been afraid of storms for as long as I can remember." I snuggle closer to him and press a hand against his chest.

His breathing becomes heavier, and the huge bulge between his legs presses into my stomach.

"Jay?"

"Stop talking, Layla," he orders me as if he knows what I'm going to ask.

I bite my lip and look up at him. He looks down at me and shakes his head, his jaw firm. "Don't look at me like that, princess. Go to sleep."

The look on his face brooks no argument, and I don't want him to change his mind about letting me sleep with him, so I decide not to push him right now. Instead, I turn in his arms until that swollen part of him is wedged up against my butt. I wiggle around, trying to get comfortable, but his arms band around me tightly.

"Stop wiggling," he grits.

I still at the tone of his voice, my entire body flushing with awareness. "Okay," I whisper.

"Go to sleep," he orders again.

My body feels alive. It's like there's a buzz running through it. I don't know if I'll be able to sleep, but I lie there savoring the feeling of Jay's arms around me and his hard chest behind me—and his huge bulge poking me in the butt. I may be a virgin, but I know what *that* means. Jay wants me, whether he'll admit it or not.

I snuggle deeper into him as drowsiness overtakes me. Before I know it, I've fallen asleep wrapped up in his big, strong arms.

four

Jay

NO SOONER DID I get my dick to go halfway down than Layla came skittering in here, setting the fucker to full mast again.

She's lying in my arms, sleeping peacefully, but there's no sleep for me. She's wearing a tank top two sizes too small for her and a pair of tiny cotton panties with cherries on them.

Motherfucking *cherries.*

All I'd need to do to sink inside her is pull those little panties to the side. She wouldn't even whimper a protest. No, she'd curl her perfect body against me and look at me with those stars in her eyes like I'm her hero instead of the dirty man stealing her innocence.

My cock twitches in my pants and I grit my teeth, grinding my molars.

As difficult as this is for my dick, I love having her sleeping form in my arms. She looks even more angelic and innocent in her sleep. Her lips are parted, her sweet breath fanning across my chest. She long since turned back to face me in her sleep and nuzzled her face against my bare chest.

Nothing in the world compares to having this angel sleeping so trustingly in my arms.

I don't know how long I stay awake, battling with my body and marveling at her softness in my arms, but I finally slip off into a doze. I awaken with a start when Layla's weight moves over me. Somehow, she's crawled right on top of me, and her sweet, young cunt is pressed right atop my rock-hard erection, hot and pulsing. She's still asleep, and I groan as all the blood in my body rushes straight to my cock.

I'm throbbing and leaking from the tip. She'll have a stain on her panties from my leaking cock, and the thought doesn't help matters because my balls grow even heavier at the image my mind has painted.

Layla moans and grinds herself on me in her sleep. My hands fly to her hips to still her movements. As much as I want to hump her sweet pussy, I refuse to violate her in her sleep.

"Jay?" her sleepy voice mumbles my name, and her eyes blink open.

Thank fuck. She's waking up.

Her sleepy eyes find mine, and she lets out a moan before she grinds herself on me again.

I can't help it. I slide against her, savoring her gasp when I stimulate her clit. She moans again and pushes herself back onto me, humping her panty-covered mound on my bulge.

I allow it for a few more moments before I finally get control of my senses enough to stop her with a hand on her hip. "Layla, princess, we can't do this."

"Why not?" she whimpers as she tries to hump me again.

My hands on her hips hold her still. "Because it's...wrong."

She shakes her head defiantly, her blonde hair bouncing with the movement. "No, it's not. We're both consenting adults. Let me make you feel good, Jay."

Fuck, she's killing me. Every muscle in my body is taut as I swallow thickly.

"I want it," she whispers, putting the final nail in my coffin.

"Fuck," I grunt as I flip her over while thrusting my hips, humping up against her. "How can I resist when your hot little cunt is pulsing right up against me?"

She whimpers a sound of victory as she lifts her hips, humping me back.

"Not gonna pop that little cherry, though," I grit as I continue to rut at her through our underwear.

She lets out a whimper of protest, but I shush her with a kiss, delving my tongue into her sweet depths.

And holy shit, she's the sweetest thing I've ever tasted. She's like sugar-covered honey. "Ah, fuck, princess, fuck. You want me to make you come?"

"Yes!"

I rub my dick along her panties, and her wetness oozes through the material onto the front of my boxers, branding my cock with her juices.

She offers her lips up to me as her breathing becomes ragged. I kiss her hungrily, my chest heaving and my arms shaking as I hump against her like a dog in heat.

My balls are churning, and I know I'm fixing to make a mess in my boxers, but I can't stop. I angle my hips to hit her clit hard one last time, and she screams, her arms and legs wrapping around me.

I keep moving, riding her through her orgasm as

my own overtakes me. I spill inside my boxers, coming harder than I've ever come, grunting and huffing and puffing like an angry bull until I collapse on the bed next to her.

She curls against my chest, and by the time I get my breath back enough to look down at her, she's already asleep.

I pass my hand over my eyes and expel a deep breath.

Fucking hell. We haven't even gotten through the first night of her living here, and I've rubbed my nasty dick all over her.

When I try to scoot away to slip out of bed, Layla protests in her sleep and clings tighter to me like I'm an enormous teddy bear she doesn't want to let go of.

Unwilling to wake her, I settle back in with my arms around her, my mind churning a thousand miles a minute as I contemplate what I'm going to do about her.

five

Jay

WE DON'T TALK about what happened the
following morning. When Layla stretches against me
like a sleepy kitten, I pull away from her and slip out
of bed.

"I'm going to take a quick shower, and then the
bathroom is all yours," I tell her gruffly.

She blinks those beautiful blue eyes and gives me
a gorgeous smile. "Good morning to you, too."

My throat is so tight I can't answer. I make my
way to the bathroom and shower in record time. I
want to make sure I give her enough time to do what-

ever high school females do to get ready in the morning.

While I get dressed, all I can think about is her naked body in my shower using my soap. Even though I rutted against her like an animal in heat last night, my dick is so hard, it's all I can do to wrangle the fucker into my pants.

I don't know what she eats for breakfast, but I whip up some French toast and eggs and lay a bowl of fruit on the table. Surprisingly, barely thirty minutes have passed when she comes skipping into the kitchen.

I almost drop the frying pan when I see what she's wearing.

She's dressed in a cheerleading uniform. The skirt is so short it barely covers her ass, and the sleeveless top is cropped right below her perky young tits, exposing her perfectly flat stomach. Her long blonde hair tumbles around her shoulders and kisses the small of her bare back, rippling with every movement she makes. She bites the elastic on her wrist, grabbing it with her teeth to pull it away before deftly gathering her long mane of hair into a ponytail and securing it with the hair tie.

I stand there slack-jawed as I stare at her, my cock as thick as a soda can about to fizz over.

My throat works before I'm finally able to speak. "What are you wearing?"

She gives me a bright smile before flouncing over and sitting at the bar. "It's my cheerleading uniform, silly. We have to wear them every Friday when there's a game."

"A cheerleader," I echo stupidly.

She nods, her ponytail bobbing up and down with the movement.

Why am I surprised she's a cheerleader?

"Oh, this looks yummy!" She beams as she looks at the food on the table.

"I didn't know what you liked, so I made a bit of everything."

She grabs a fork and digs in. "I love everything." She's so happy and breezy and eager to please. Fuck, she's like a ray of sunshine.

"Oh, before I forget. This is for you." I hold out the gold chain.

Layla's eyes widen. "You got me a necklace?"

I grunt. "It was my mother's, but I thought you could put your mother's ring on it so it doesn't keep falling off your finger."

She beams up at me. "Oh, my god, Jay. It's beautiful. I'll treasure it forever."

I watch as she slips the ring onto the chain and struggles to clasp it behind her neck.

"Here." I offer to help her.

She holds her hair up, and I clasp the necklace onto her neck, trying not to get turned on by the beautiful column of her throat. I swallow as my eyes trail over her barely covered form. I don't like this cheerleading outfit *at all*. She looks too delectable in it, and I was a teenage boy once. I know the filthy thoughts that go through their heads when they see her like this. Hell, I'm a grown man, and I know what I'm thinking looking at her like this. My hands ball into fists at the thought.

Her sweet voice breaks into my brooding. "Will you come?"

I nearly choke, descending into a coughing fit. I grab my glass of water and take a swig to clear my throat before I gape at her. "Excuse me?"

Her head is cocked to the side as she looks at me oddly. "To the football game tonight?" She speaks slowly. "I was asking if you would come watch me cheer."

Jesus, I must have missed the first half of her question, too absorbed in how she looks in that cheerleading outfit. My chest tightens. She wants me to watch her cheer. I force myself to act nonchalant as I fork a bite of eggs into my mouth. "Did your father go to your games?"

Her smile falters as she looks down. "Actually, no. Dad could hardly ever come. He was always too busy."

Sadness descends over her like a dark cloud, and my chest squeezes harder. I can't stand seeing her so downcast. "If you want me there, I'll be there," I finally grunt.

It's like all the clouds have rolled out, and the sun is shining in full force again. She turns her head to me, her eyes beaming. "Yay!" she exclaims with a little clap of her hands.

I tell myself I'm only going to support her and keep an eye out for her. I might not be her legal guardian, but I have to make sure no one messes with her. It has nothing to do with me wanting an excuse to stare at her as she bounces her body all over a football field in that tiny outfit.

Absolutely nothing at all.

Layla

This day has been beautiful. The sun is shining so brightly. There's no trace of the storm from last night.

I felt as special as the Queen of England when Jay dropped me off at school this morning. I felt his eyes on me the entire way to the front door, and when I turned around, he was staring at me with those black shades on, his big shoulders straining at the seams of his white button-up shirt.

He told me he would be here after school to pick me up. Jay is a car salesman, and from what I understand, he's a damn good one because he can set his hours and come and go as he pleases, even though he doesn't own the lot where he works.

I float from class to class all day, and the closer it gets to time for the bell to ring, the more my tummy flutters. I finger the necklace he gave me. I can't believe he gave me a necklace that was his mother's. That only makes it more special to me. I love feeling the slight weight of it around my neck. It makes me feel like I have a piece of him with me. I'm so excited about seeing Jay again.

I go through the motions of leading the squad throughout the pep rally. I might be the tiniest cheer-leader on the squad and the one who's always thrown up in the air and placed on the top of the pyramid, but I'm also the captain. I'm naturally flexible and athletic, and I've worked hard for my spot on this squad all four years of my high school career.

I'm brimming with excitement that Jay has agreed to come watch me cheer. All the other girls always have family in the stands to support them, but I never have. My dad was always too busy chasing his next get-rich-quick scheme. I asked him to come to games repeatedly, but he always came up with excuses why he couldn't, so I eventually stopped asking him.

But not Jay. My heart swells. He agreed to come see me.

My heart does a flip when I walk out and see Jay's SUV idling by the sidewalk. His eyes instantly find me, and I skip over to the SUV.

Jay gets out and opens my door for me before I get there. I hear several girls tittering behind me, and it's no wonder. Jay is nothing like the boys here at the high school. He's big and bulky. A *man*.

They can eat their hearts out because he's *mine*.

"Hey, Layla!" I hear Landon screaming my name. I stop and glance over my shoulder to look at him. "See you at the game tonight, gorgeous!" He winks at me.

"See ya!" I wave back at him with a bright smile.

When I turn and look at Jay, my smile falters. The look he's giving Landon could cut glass. He turns those stormy eyes on me, his lips pressed into a thin line. "Get in the car."

I swallow and scurry to obey. Good lord, Jay looks angry. I don't understand why, but it makes those butterflies in my stomach flutter faster.

Like he did yesterday, Jay leans into the car and buckles me up before closing the door and stalking around to the driver's side. He gets in and slams his door before he tips his head toward Landon and asks, "Who's that?"

"That's Landon. He's the captain of the football team."

Jay's hands tighten on the steering wheel before he throws the car into gear and takes off, the tires squealing as he does so.

He takes off so fast my back is thrown against the seat. "Jay, what's wrong?"

Jay's chest heaves, and his nostrils flare. His jaw is so tight it looks like it could shatter. "I want you to stay away from him."

"Who? Landon?"

Jay grinds his molars together when I say Landon's name.

"He's my friend, Jay."

Jay lets out a laugh devoid of humor. "That *boy* has more than friendship on his mind."

His tone is filled with so much fury it gives me pause. A rush of pleasure runs through me when I realize what's going on. Jay is *jealous.* It shouldn't make me as happy as it does, but I'm over the moon, though I make sure not to let Jay know.

I suppress my smile. "Okay."

Jay blinks in surprise. "Okay?" He raises a disbelieving eyebrow like he expected me to put up a bigger fight.

I shrug. "Yeah. I trust you. If you tell me to stay away from him, I will."

He pauses, nods his head approvingly, and turns back to the road. "Good girl."

Oh. My. God. I smash my thighs together to try to alleviate the sudden ache there. My breath hitches and Jay looks over at me. His eyes darken as they flick to my thighs pressed tightly together.

He makes a noise like a half-growl, half-grunt, and reaches down to adjust himself. The sight of Jay touching the huge bulge in his pants and knowing I'm the one responsible has me ready to combust. I'm hot all over and aware of a pulsing deep within my body.

I can't wait to get back to the house. Maybe I can coax Jay into rubbing himself against me again like he did last night.

It's embarrassing, but last night was my first

orgasm. I've tried touching myself in the past, but I could never reach that pinnacle—not how I did with Jay. Even if I'd been able to make myself come, it would never feel the way it did with Jay rubbing himself against me. I'm wet thinking about it.

To my consternation, Jay doesn't turn in at his house. He keeps driving until we reach a diner.

"Need to make sure you're fed before your big game tonight," he says when he catches me watching him.

I'm not stupid. Jay is afraid to be alone with me. He's afraid of what he might do. I lower my head to hide my smile.

Until later then...

six

Jay

WATCHING Layla eat is an erotic experience in and of itself. Hell, everything this girl does has me ready to bust in my pants. I couldn't focus on making a sale today because I was thinking of her in that tight cheerleading outfit, knowing all the boys were creaming in their pants over her.

My hands ball into fists on the table as I remember the young prick talking to her and how he looked at her. I saw the filthy thoughts in his head.

"Are you okay?" Layla asks me before she takes a sip of her strawberry milkshake, her big blue eyes staring at me while she sucks the straw, her cheeks hollowing. I imagine replacing the straw with my cock and those blue eyes gazing up at me with my swollen flesh halfway down her throat.

"No," I finally grunt out honestly.

She stops with a fry halfway to her mouth and frowns at me prettily. "Is there anything I can do?"

"Yes," I bark at her impatiently. "Eat your food."

She blinks at me, the hurt instantly transforming her face. Tears shimmer in her eyes, and she lowers her lashes, hiding herself from me.

I'm instantly chagrined, and a sharp pang shoots through my chest.

"Fuck, Layla." I run a hand through my hair. "I'm sorry, princess. It's been a rough day."

She peeks at me from beneath her lowered lashes when I call her princess. "When we get home later, I'll give you a massage and help rub some tension out of you," she offers sweetly.

I close my eyes and fight back a groan. Fuck, this girl is every man's wet dream. Young, innocent, barely legal, cheerleader, virgin, masseuse. I'm confident there's no fantasy she can't fulfill. "We'll talk about it later."

She smiles and finishes her cheeseburger and fries. I readjust my dick under the table and try my best not to watch her as she slurps on the strawberry milk-shake, closing her eyes and moaning as she does so.

Sweet Jesus, it's no wonder her father wouldn't let her date. If she went out with a boy and acted like this, he'd maul her before the night was over, whether she wanted it or not.

When we've eaten, I pay the check, and we head back to school for the football game.

Layla is buzzing with excitement. She directs me to a seat in the front of the stands where the cheer-leaders' families usually sit. My chest squeezes again when I see how proud she is to have me there. It makes me want to go down to the jail and kick Doug's ass for never supporting her.

When the other cheerleaders ask her who she has with her, she introduces me proudly as her friend, Jay. My heart aches for her. Thank god she doesn't intro-duce me as her uncle because my thoughts about her are far from uncle-ish.

I used to play football in high school, and while I'm still a fan of the sport, I don't spare a glance at the field. I can't tell you which team is winning or which players show the most potential because my eyes are glued on my princess the whole time. She's always front and center of the squad, leading them in their cheers, looking pretty as a button as she swings her hips, kicks her legs, and sashays around the field. She jumps up and down excitedly when the team scores a touchdown, shaking those pom-poms and flipping her ponytail all over the place. She dazzles the crowd with her gorgeous smile. When halftime comes and the cheerleaders take the field to do their halftime performance, I'm clapping and whistling louder than anyone in support of her.

Layla's eyes seek me out throughout the night. She looks right into my eyes as she shakes her butt and pops her hips. I pray to God nobody looks over at me and sees the huge boner tenting my pants. They'd probably charge me and ban me from school grounds forever. By the end of the game, I'm so wound up, the barest breeze could set me off.

I leave the stands and head down to the field to get Layla and escort her back to the vehicle when I see that arrogant prick in his football uniform, his hair sweaty, walking over to my princess with a big grin on his face. He's holding his football helmet under his arm with one hand. The other arm, he wraps around Layla's shoulders. He looks down at her and says something. I'm too far away to hear, but I don't care what the fuck he's saying to her.

I'm no longer in control of myself. I'm on the field

in a flash, yanking his arm from around her shoulders. "Don't fucking touch her!"

He blinks and steps back with a hand up in the air. "Whoa, dude! Chill out!"

My chest heaves as I contemplate all the ways I can murder this kid.

Layla calms me with a gentle hand on my chest. Her touch captures my attention, and I look into her big blue eyes.

"It's okay, Jay," she tells me gently. "Take me home." When my eyes cut back up to look at the young prick, she adds, "Please."

Fuck. I can't deny her when she says "please" in that sweet voice. So instead of throttling this fucker to within an inch of his life, I grab Layla's hand and yank her off the football field. She trails along beside me willingly. She's silent as I buckle her into my vehicle before getting in and slamming the door. I'm seething with rage at the memory of that boy's arm around her.

Layla must sense my volatile temperament because, for once, she keeps her mouth shut.

Neither of us speaks until we're in my house.

"Jay," she says my name softly, hesitantly.

I'm still strung too tight. I shake my head at her firmly. "Go to your room, Layla."

Her mouth drops open in shock, and her eyes flash with anger. She crosses her arms over her chest and glares at me. "You can't tell me what to do," she smarts off like a little brat.

A warning growl tears up my throat. "Watch me."

She purses her lips and continues to glare at me. I shove my fingers through my hair before I point to her room and say sternly, "If you don't go to your room right fucking now, Layla, I swear to God, I'm going to throw you over my knee and spank that beautiful little bottom."

Her mouth goes slack for a moment, and her cheeks flush. All my senses are on high alert as I see the look that passes over her eyes. Something about that idea doesn't completely repulse her. No, if I'm not mistaken, a part of her *likes* the idea of me spanking her. *Fuuuck.* My already hard cock swells even harder.

She uncrosses her arms and turns on her heel, angrily flipping her hair behind her shoulder. She glances back at me and hisses, "Fine, Daddy."

I go completely still.

Layla's eyes widen, and her mouth parts slightly as her breathing speeds up.

Hearing her call me *Daddy* unleashes something inside me. It's like a match on kerosene. I burn all over.

I'm on her in an instant, snarling and growling at her like a rabid beast as I hump her pussy through her cheerleading skirt. "You've been a very bad girl." I grab handfuls of her ass and pull her tighter against me as I continue to ride her through our clothes. "Walking around in this cheerleading outfit all day, driving Daddy crazy like a nasty little cock tease."

Layla gasps, but I don't know if it's from revulsion at my filthy words or because she likes it. I'm too gone to care. "I bet your virgin pussy is sopping wet, isn't it?"

She whimpers and presses herself closer to me, rubbing her chest against me, drawing my attention to her breasts.

I yank her top up like a savage and moan at the sight of her perfect breasts, the nipples hardened into peaks. "You want Daddy to suck these?"

I don't wait for her answer before I fall on her breasts, worshipping them with kisses and licks and nips and then more licks to chase away the sting of my teeth.

And Christ, if she isn't arching her sweet body and offering herself to me.

I can't take it anymore and reach under her skirt, pushing the liner to the side to feel the moisture between her legs. She's fucking soaked.

The evidence of her arousal causes a rope of precum to shoot from my tip. "Fuck, Layla," I groan as I drop to my knees and pull the cheerleading skirt down her legs. "Gotta taste this sweet thing. Look at it dripping wet for Daddy. You want Daddy to lick it for you, princess?"

I look up at her, and her eyes are glazed. She fists her hands in my hair, and then I'm devouring her, licking and sucking and slurping on her pussy like I'm a man on death row and she's my last meal. "I've never tasted anything this sweet in all my life, princess. Swear to God."

I've been eating her for less than a minute when her legs tense. "Jay!" She screams my name and floods my face with her sweet release.

"Fuck yes," I groan as I unzip my pants. My cock falls into my hand, hot and heavy. I stroke it viciously. My balls are so full they feel like they're going to bubble over at any moment. "Princess," I growl and pant, "this pretty little pussy is gonna make Daddy come."

Layla lets out another whimper. It's the sexiest sound I've ever heard.

I stagger to my feet, pumping my cock furiously as it spurts all over her stomach. I aim it down and spray her mound with copious amounts of my cum. It's a caveman move, but it fills me with satisfaction to see her pussy covered in my seed.

When I finally stop coming and regain my senses, my gaze finds Layla. She's staring up at me in shock, her mouth hanging open.

Reality comes crashing back down on me. I'm disgusted with myself. My god, did I really just speak all that filth to her? Calling myself her daddy and jerking off all over her?

I can't look at her as I promptly zip myself back up and take off to my bedroom. I need to put as much distance as I can between Layla and me before I lose it and do what I've been dying to do since the moment I first laid eyes on her—jam myself so deep inside her she'll never be able to think about another man.

seven

Layla

I'M horny and pissed and frustrated and confused and so mad at Jay I want to slap him.

My shoulders slump. No, I don't want to slap him. I want him to talk to me. I want him to hold me. I want him to fuck me and make me a woman, make me *his*.

I was giving him attitude when I called him Daddy last night, but something clicked within me as soon as the word left my mouth. Something deep and dark and forbidden.

It felt right to call Jay Daddy. I don't know where

this is coming from. It's not like I have deep-seated daddy issues, but Jay is my daddy. The man who takes care of me. The man I want to run to when there's a storm. The man who gets me so hot and bothered I'm tossing and turning and aching all night.

And he liked me calling him daddy as much as I did. There was this animalistic look in his eye—like he couldn't control himself.

I loved it.

He was finally going to give us what we both wanted. He called himself my daddy, spoke such deliciously filthy things in my ear and marked me with his cum. It was hot and raw and primal, and then he stormed off to his room, and I haven't seen him since.

He's locked me out, no doubt convincing himself that what's between us is wrong.

But it's not wrong. I'll never believe that. It's just *us*. Jay and I have a connection. It pulses between us like a live wire. It sparked to life the moment he showed up to get me and bring me to live with him. It doesn't make sense, and it doesn't have to. I don't care. I can't fight this, and I'm tired of Jay fighting it.

He thinks he's too old for me. He feels guilty because I'm his friend's daughter. He thinks he's taking advantage of me since I live with him.

But it's not true. I see the way he looks at me. I know he feels the same way I do.

When morning rolls around and he still hasn't emerged from his room, I decide to take matters into my own hands. If he wants to lock himself away from me, I'll be a little brat. I'll push him if that's what it takes. If getting him angry is the only way to get his hands on me, that's what I'll do.

I rifle through my bags and smile when I find what I'm looking for. I put on the tiny scraps of fabric. Jay is not going to be okay with me going out looking like this, no matter that it's a bikini and entirely appropriate for the beach.

I flounce out of my room, letting the door fall shut heavily. I don't stomp through the house, but I allow my footsteps to fall harder than they usually do. Heading into the kitchen, I take my time pouring a glass of orange juice. I open and close a few drawers and cabinets, letting them fall shut instead of gently closing them. I want to make my presence known without being too obvious.

It's Saturday, and I'm not sure how late Jay sleeps in on the weekends, but he'll have to come out of his bedroom sooner or later. I'd prefer it be sooner.

I sit at the barstool and slowly sip my orange juice, trying to make the glass last so I have a reason to be sitting here when he gets up. Fortunately, I don't have to wait long.

My heart jumps into my throat when Jay walks into the kitchen. He takes one glance at me, and his eyes widen comically before his mouth presses into a firm line. I fight back the grin threatening to spill across my face as he shakes his head.

His gray eyes are stormy and promising thunder. "No way." His voice is gruff.

I raise an eyebrow. "What?" I ask innocently.

"Absolutely not," he growls as he stalks over to the counter and plants his hands on it, staring at me. "There's no way you're going out like that."

I shrug. "Like what?"

"In those two scraps of fabric."

"Oh, you mean a bikini?" I keep my eyes wide and innocent before I add, "Because this is what girls wear when they go to the beach, Jay, and I'm going to the beach."

I leave the discarded orange juice on the counter as I hop off the barstool and start walking away from him.

A rumble sounds in his chest. "You're not walking out of this house dressed like that. I don't give a fuck where you're going."

I glance back at him in disinterest. "Yes, I am, Jay.

But if you're so concerned, you're more than welcome to come with me."

I turn to walk away, but he makes a feral sound, and I'm suddenly spun around. His big hands land on my shoulders, and his gray eyes blaze down at me. "You little brat. I'm going to do what I should have done last night."

Before I can say or do anything, he pulls me over to the counter and sits abruptly on the barstool, yanking me into his lap and bending me over his knee. I gasp and cling to his leg as he tugs down my bikini bottoms and plants a hard smack right on my ass.

I yelp in shock at the sting, but his hand smooths over my bottom, rubbing away the pain. He smacks my ass again and rubs away the sting.

It's degrading. It's humiliating.

And I love it.

I moan as wetness gushes between my thighs.

"Is this what you wanted?" He smacks my ass again and soothes my hot skin.

His hard erection pokes into my side, and I moan deeper as my head falls forward. I push my ass out, anticipating another slap.

He doesn't disappoint me. I bite my lip to hold in my moan this time.

His breath comes out in labored pants as he marvels, "You like this, don't you?"

I can't answer.

He lifts my chin and bends to look at me, prompting me for an answer. "Don't you, princess?"

I close my eyes in shame. "Yes."

He groans and delivers another stinging slap before soothing it away. The fifth slap is what finally does it. I burst into tears, and quick as a flash, he has me sitting across his lap, gathering me into his arms.

"Sshh," he hushes me as he runs his fingers through my hair and along my back. I cling to him, sobbing into his neck, though I don't know why I'm breaking down like this. I'm not upset or angry with him. I just feel so *much*. I can't contain it all.

He seems to understand because he strokes me and whispers words of praise into my ear. "Such a perfect little princess. You make Daddy so proud."

He soothes me until my tears are spent. When I finally raise my head, Jay is looking down at me tenderly. He cups my face and strokes his thumb over my cheek. "Feel better?"

I nod, biting my lip. "Will you kiss me, Daddy?"

He makes a choked sound as he stares down at me. I lick my lips, praying he won't shut us down now. His eyes move to my lips, and he descends upon me.

He fists his hands in my hair as he angles my head and plunders my mouth hungrily like a beast let out of his cage.

I sigh and melt into him.

"Fuck," he whispers against my lips. "Can't fight it anymore. Want you. Need you."

"I need you too, Daddy," I whisper against his lips.

Like last night, that word seems to detonate something inside him. He shoves his tongue inside my mouth and growls into the kiss. His growl rumbles into my chest and sets my soul on fire.

"Going to give you what you want, baby doll. You've been aching for Daddy's dick since I brought you into this house, haven't you?"

I moan and wrap my arms around his neck. He trails kisses along my jaw and to the side of my neck, where he licks and sucks. I've never had a hickey before, and I know everyone at school will tease me about it, but I don't give a fuck. I'll wear Jay's marks with pride.

Jay. *Daddy.*

Jay pushes my bikini bottoms off and unsnaps the back of my bandeau top bikini. It falls to the floor between us, and Jay pulls down his shorts. His thick erection springs out and bobs in the air. I stare at it in awe before reaching down and tentatively stroking it.

I gasp. It amazes me how it's so hard yet so velvety soft.

Jay throws his head back and moans as he grabs my hand and pulls me gently down onto his lap.

"We're gonna play a game, princess." His voice is low and gruff, and my heart flutters at his tone.

"Okay," I whisper.

"Good girl," he praises me, and I bite my lip as more moisture pools between my legs.

His eyes darken when he sees it sliding down the inside of my thigh. He inhales a shaky breath before saying, "You're going to sit here on Daddy's lap and bounce around."

I fall into my role easily. I bite my lip nervously as I look down at his big cock jutting from between his legs. "But, Daddy, your thing... will it get in the way?"

Jay's nostrils flare and sweat breaks out on his brow. "No, princess. It's going to be inside you."

I furrow my brow. "Inside me?" I look down at his swollen length. "Are you sure it will fit?" I'm not entirely playacting. I have my doubts, but my body tells me it wants to try, even if Jay splits me in half.

Jay nods his head. "Here. Let me show you."

He guides me astride him and lines himself up with my hole. The large crown pushes inside me, and I tense involuntarily. I hold onto his shoulders tightly.

Jay's chest heaves as he grips my hips. He catches my gaze. "Are you sure you want to do this, Layla?"

I nod my head vigorously. "Yes, Jay. I want this. I want you. I want *us*."

Jay's cock jumps as he guides me gently down onto him. He pushes slowly into me, stretching and filling me so completely, but he's so big, I pant with the effort to take him in.

When he reaches my hymen, he stops, and I sit there, suspended, as we look into each other's eyes.

"Are you ready, princess?"

I bite my lip and give him a nod.

He holds my eyes as he pulls me down onto him while thrusting deep with his hips, taking my virginity once and for all.

I scream, and he groans. I fall onto him, wrapping my arms tightly around his neck and burrowing my face in his chest, whimpering at the sting.

"Fuck, Layla. You feel incredible," he groans into my ear.

I clench around him involuntarily, and he makes a choked sound. "I can't believe that hot little thing is pulsing around me so tight."

I wiggle on top of him, struggling to get more comfortable. Another groan rips up from his chest.

"Fuck, princess. Gotta move. You think you can bounce up and down on Daddy's dick?"

I lift my hips up and down, trying my best to do as he asks. "Like that, Daddy?"

He throws his head back, the muscles in his neck cording, "Fuck, yes. Just like that, baby doll."

I bounce up and down on him while he holds my hips and thrusts into me. He's hitting something deep inside me, causing tingles to shoot through my entire body. It's almost ticklish like I'm going to pee.

"Jay," I groan his name and cover his hands with mine.

Jay picks up the pace, hammering his hips up into me. "Yes, Layla. Come for me, angel princess. Cream all over your daddy's big dick. Be a good girl, and Daddy will give you all his nasty cum."

Jay's filthy words send me flying over the edge. My entire body seizes up as my pussy flutters around him. I scream as a white-hot ecstasy pours through my body.

"Fuck, Layla!" Jay shouts as he continues to rut up into me with jerky movements. He roars and finally stills, his arms banding around my back and pressing me close. Hot liquid spurts deep inside me as Jay grunts and groans like a big bear. His body jerks as he spurts rope after rope of fiery heat into me, branding me, marking me as his own.

I slump against him, burrowing my head in his neck, completely spent and happier than I can ever remember.

His hands pet over my head as he murmurs praises in my ear. "Good girl. So beautiful when you come for Daddy. Took Daddy's dick like such a big girl. Daddy's perfect little angel princess. Going to take care of you forever. You're mine now, Layla."

His words are like a balm to my heart. I smile against his neck.

The last thing I remember before I fall asleep in his arms is him pressing a tender kiss to the side of my forehead.

eight

Layla

IT'S like a switch has been flipped. Jay is loving and possessive and downright obsessive over me, and I love every second of it. He can't seem to keep his hands off me.

We fall completely into our roles whenever we play. It might not be normal. Hell, I don't know what normal is since Jay is my first everything, but I know what works for us, and I don't care what anyone thinks. Jay is my daddy in the bedroom, and I love being his little girl. Nothing turns us on more.

I don't sleep in my bedroom anymore. Jay

promptly moved me into his room, where he sleeps with his arms and legs around me all night. I love it. He's like my very own blanket of pure man.

Jay fucks me every morning before I go to school. He forbids me to wash his cum out of my pussy, saying he likes the thought of his seed between my legs all day. He says it'll remind me I belong to him when boys hit on me. It's so hot feeling Jay's cum leaking out of me, and I'm always soaking wet and ready for round two by the time he picks me up after school.

And he never fails to deliver. Sometimes he has me bounce up and down on his lap like our first time. Other times, he rails me missionary style, grunting and growling over me like a horny bear. And then there are the times he gets me on all fours and pulls my ponytail while he rides me from behind, slapping my ass as he does so.

Sometimes I'm a very good girl, and he rewards me with a "lollipop." I can't believe how much I love his salty, musky taste. Jay is so big I can hardly fit the tip in my mouth, but he praises me for my efforts and teaches me how to use my hands to give him blowjobs. I especially love it when he holds me upside down and eats my pussy while I suck on him. I love it when he loses control, cursing and speaking filth while he comes down my throat. It fills me with such a rush of feminine power. I love making my daddy feel good.

But other times, I'm a bad girl on purpose and push him until he drags me over his knee and reddens my bottom until I'm dripping wet. Then he fucks me voraciously until I can't see straight. I might be nearly half his age, but Jay is a vital alpha male. No sooner does he come in me than I'm like a limp rag doll, but his cock is always immediately hard and ready to go again at a moment's notice.

We've even started to take our role-playing outside the bedroom. When we share meals at home, Jay pulls me onto his knee and feeds me. There's something so intimate about the way he takes care of me. He loves cooking for me and feeding me from his hand while he strokes my hair and rubs my back. He also likes to wash me, so I don't shower alone anymore. No, Jay insists on washing every square inch of my body for me, and I'd be lying if I said I don't love his fingers gently massaging my head when he washes my hair. He knows exactly how to make me purr like a contented feline.

He hasn't bought me shampoo because he admitted he likes knowing I'm walking around with his scent all over me. It's barbaric and primitive, but it calls to something deep inside me and makes my stomach clench.

When it comes to my cheerleading, Jay is more supportive than my father ever was. He never misses a game. He's always sitting front and center, watching me the entire time. I want to tell all the girls at school he's my boyfriend, but Jay cautions me against it, telling me some people won't understand our dynamic. I've almost slipped up and called him Daddy in public several times but caught myself in time.

I know Jay is right, and the world won't understand us, but we get each other, and we love the way we play. It works for us, and no one will convince me it's wrong.

Everything is going perfectly. It's Jay and me in our own world—until the day my father shows up on Jay's doorstep.

"Doug!" I hear Jay's shocked voice from where I'm sitting in the living room. Jay and I were cuddled up on the couch, watching a movie.

I'm sure my dad can't hear it, but there's a note of panic in Jay's voice. I frown, an ominous feeling washing over me.

"Hey, man! Yeah, they let me out early for good behavior. Can you believe it?" He laughs.

Jay invites my father in and enters the living room

with a somber look.

"How have you two been getting along?" Dad asks Jay. "She hasn't been giving you too much trouble, has she? I know she can be a handful."

"She's definitely a handful," Jay agrees.

I smile at my father and then look at Jay, but he won't meet my eyes. My smile falters.

My dad, oblivious to the tension between Jay and me, opens his arms for a hug. I step into his embrace, feeling like a shitty daughter for thinking my dad came at a bad time. I should be glad he's out of jail. I *am* glad he's out of jail.

I'm ashamed of how little I thought about him when he was locked up. I was so wrapped up in Jay, but in my defense, my dad and I haven't been close since Mom died. He tries to be a good father, but he's never been there for me the way Jay has.

And now I'm worried my dad showing up will change things between Jay and me, especially with the way Jay is acting right now.

"So, man, I know I've already put you out enough having you watch my daughter while I was locked up, but do you think I could crash here for a day or two until I get Layla and me a new place?"

I blink, and my eyes snap to my father. Of course, he assumes I want to live with him now he's out. I bite my lip and look at Jay, who's studiously avoiding my gaze.

"Of course." Jay's voice is flat when he agrees.

My heart drops. Is he not going to fight for us? Is it all over now that my dad is out? Does Jay not plan on telling my dad about us? I'm eighteen, so legally, I can be with whoever I want. I know Jay wants me. I saw how happy he was when it was the two of us in our little bubble, but now he's breaking my heart.

He knows it, too, because he can't even bear to look at me.

My dad plops down on the couch and chats away, talking about his time in jail and his plans for the future. How he's going to do better. How he'll never fuck up again.

Jay and I are both silent. I cast glances at him, but he hasn't looked at me since my father walked in the door.

As I sit there, silently begging Jay to look at me, my hurt turns to anger.

Jay knows me well enough to realize I act out when I'm angry. I excuse myself from the room, feeling the heat of Jay's eyes boring into my back. He couldn't meet my eyes head-on, but he'll stare a hole in my back as I walk away. Fuck him.

I flounce into the bedroom I haven't slept in since

Jay and I gave in to our passion. It's become a storage space for my clothes where I come every morning to grab some clothes.

I rifle through my garments now, looking for the skimpiest, sluttiest outfit I can find. A micro mini skirt and a V-neck top, both of which are two sizes too small for me. I grew out of them sophomore year, but I can still squeeze into them and show off plenty of cleavage and leg.

I survey my appearance in the mirror and decide I look perfect for hitting up a club. In fact, there's one down the street that the squad has been begging me to go to with them.

Jay won't look at me, so I should be able to walk out of the house dressed like this, right? And he won't dare say anything in front of my father because he doesn't want Dad to know about our relationship. He's ashamed of us.

A pang of guilt hits me because I know I'm only doing this to goad him, but dammit, he hurt me. It hurts that he won't look at me. I thought what we had was special, but Jay is treating me like a dirty little secret, and it cuts me to the quick.

I wipe the angry tears from my face, apply a heavy eyeliner, and swipe on some mascara. I top off the look with fire engine red lipstick and let my hair hang long down my back. It feels sensuous, falling over my bare back and shoulders.

I throw on a pair of sky-high heels the other cheerleaders talked me into buying eons ago but have rarely worn. I can walk in heels, but I'm not a huge fan of them, even though they make my legs look amazing.

When I'm done primping, I flounce out of my room and down the hallway through the living room to the front door. I instantly feel Jay's eyes on me, and he makes a strangled sound.

"Where you heading off to, Layla? Is there a party tonight?" Dad asks.

I smile brightly, making sure to meet Jay's gaze. He's certainly looking at me now. My tummy flutters when I see his clenched jaw, and his eyes shoot fire at me.

I toss my head defiantly. "Yeah, I'm meeting some of the squad at this club right down the street. It's eighteen and up night. Don't worry. I don't have a fake ID, so there won't be any drinking."

My dad nods, accepting my answer. "Okay, Laylabug. Call if you need us."

Jay looks like his eyes are about to pop out of his head. His nostrils flare, and his hands ball into fists as he turns his head to my father. "Are you going to let her go out dressed like that?"

I don't try to hide my smirk when Dad gives Jay a questioning look and shrugs. "Layla is eighteen, and she's always been a responsible girl. I trust her. Besides, I couldn't stop her even if I wanted to. She's legally an adult now and can do what she wants."

I give Jay a smug smile before I march out the front door without saying another word to him.

The smug smile falls from my face as soon as I walk out the door, and I'm pensive as I traipse down the street to the club.

My victory feels hollow. I didn't like the disappointment and outrage on Jay's face. He hurt me, but hurting him back doesn't feel good. I'm behaving immaturely, and my cheeks flush in shame.

Maybe Jay is right. Maybe I am too young for him. Look at how I behaved. I didn't act like a grown woman at all. I acted like a brat throwing a temper tantrum.

Tears prick at my eyes, but I blink them back and straighten my shoulders. Oh well. What's done is done. My heart may be breaking, but I'm determined to see this night through now. Maybe I can dance away all thoughts of Jay.

I know one thing. I refuse to go back to the house with my tail between my legs so Jay can pretend I don't exist when we're in my father's presence.

nine

Layla

I'VE BEEN on the dance floor for two minutes when I hear someone shouting my name. A shiver passes through me. No, it can't be.

Daddy.

I stop mid-dance. I've been dancing with the other cheerleaders on the squad, trying to lose myself in the music even though my heart isn't in it.

"Layla!" I hear my name yelled over the music again and turn to see Jay pushing his way through the throng of teenagers toward me.

My heart gallops in my chest at the sight of him,

but his rejection when my father showed up still burns. I turn and push my way through the crowd, away from him.

"Layla!"

I pause at his stern tone, another shiver wracking my body. That's his *daddy* voice.

"Stop right now!" His voice is dripping with authority.

I glance over my shoulder to see he's nearly upon me. It's no use. He's so big, and I'm so tiny. His long strides measure three or four of mine. I'll never be able to outrun him, so I reluctantly obey him, stopping and crossing my arms as I turn to glare at him. As he gets closer, I drop my arms to my sides and gasp when his face comes into view. The lights are flashing, and it's dimly lit in here, but I can clearly see the black eye he's sporting.

"Oh my god, Jay! What happened?" Concern for him causes all my anger to evaporate.

"I told your father about us."

I wince. "He did this to you?"

Jay shrugs. "I had it coming. I gave him a clean shot. Figured I owed him that much."

"Jay." My voice breaks and my heart squeezes at the thought of him giving up his friendship with my dad because of me. I shake my head, my shoulders slumping. "I don't want to come between you and my father. You've been friends since college." Even if they didn't see each other much, they've always kept in touch.

Jay shakes his head and cups my cheeks with his big paws. "Don't worry, Layla. It's not your problem. Your father will have to get over it, and if he doesn't, so be it. Nothing in this world is worth losing you. If I have to choose, I choose you a million times, princess."

My heart softens at his words. I search his eyes and see he means every one of them. "Jay." I tremble, my voice shaking.

His eyes swoop over me, darkening when he takes in what I'm wearing again. "Your father might be okay with you leaving the house dressed like that, but your *daddy* sure as hell isn't," he growls at me.

Heat unfurls in my belly, and my toes curl in my stilettos. "My daddy?" I whisper weakly, shocked he's daring to say it in a public place like this where anyone could hear us—even over the loud music.

"That's right." He holds my eyes. "You know who your daddy is, angel princess."

I whimper as my knees fail and fall out underneath me. Jay catches me against his chest before he tips my chin up and kisses me in the middle of the dance floor in front of everyone.

He claims my lips possessively, giving no thought to the surrounding people. His heavy erection presses into me, reaffirming how much he wants me. I whimper and push myself against him, needing to be closer, closer.

Jay must feel the same way because suddenly his hands are on my ass, lifting me until my legs wrap around his waist and his huge, swollen length pulses against my core. He pulls the hem of my miniscule skirt down, clasping his hands under it to hide my bare ass cheeks in the skimpy thong I'm wearing.

"You feel how hard you make Daddy, you naughty little girl?" he whispers in my ear. "Got Daddy popping a boner and leaking precum for you in front of all these people, needing to fuck your little princess cunt."

I whimper and burrow my head in his neck as his words send fire licking through my veins. "And you know it too," he rasps against my ear. "You were a naughty girl to tease Daddy and drive him insane."

I'm a big ball of need, humping his hips in front of everyone, but I don't care, and neither does Jay.

I moan and ask him tremulously, "Can we play ride the pony when we get home, Daddy?"

Jay twitches against me, and he tips my chin up, heat blazing from his eyes. "Yes, baby doll, once I've spanked your little ass red for leaving the house dressed like this and worrying Daddy. For getting him so hard he can't think straight."

I shake with lust, and my eyes fill with tears. My heart is so full of emotion, I can't contain it. "I love you, Jay," I whisper against his lips.

"I love you too, Layla," he growls, his lips sliding against mine. "Now, be a good girl and let Daddy take you home."

I wrap my arms tighter around his neck as he carries me out, wrapped up safe and secure in his arms.

Anywhere is home so long as I'm with Jay.

My *daddy*.

epilogue

Four Years Later

Jay

I WATCH my wife as she waves goodbye to her last client of the day. When Layla graduated from high school, she went on to get her certificate in massage therapy, and now she practices in the studio I set up for her in our home.

I sold my house to her dad and moved us out of the city. We're outside the hustle and bustle but close enough for people from the city to reach our property, where I now have an at-home car lot.

I couldn't handle being away from my angel princess for long, and working from home means we can be near one another. Besides, I can't chance leaving my baby doll alone with the men who book massages from her.

While it's difficult for me to allow her to massage other men, I knew I couldn't forbid her from doing what she loves. Layla loves her work and making her clients feel good, and I have to say she's great at what she does.

If I let her, she'd give me a massage every night. Of course, her tiny hands kneading all over me always leads to more than a massage. I end up with my dick deep inside her while I suck on her pretty titties and fuck her like I'm trying to break her little hole once and for all.

Thank god Layla loves it when I'm animalistic because she makes me so hot I can't control myself around her. Every time I tell myself I'm going to go slow and be gentle, her pussy milks me and she calls me Daddy. She looks at me with those innocent blue eyes, and I lose it, pounding into her like a rabid beast.

We've never used protection—not even the first

time I took her. I can't bear the thought of anything between us, so it's no wonder we're expecting our second child. I love the sight of Layla's tummy swollen with my seed. There's nothing hotter than seeing her pregnant and knowing I'm the one who bred her.

Doug finally came around to the idea of Layla and I being together. After seeing how in love we are, he grudgingly admitted that no one would take better care of her than me.

It didn't hurt that we gave him a grandchild pretty quickly. Doug is a huge softie for our little boy. In fact, he's keeping him this weekend so Layla and I can have some alone time.

Doug made some bad financial decisions in the past, but he's a great caretaker and a wonderful grandparent. We know our boy is safe in his hands. Doug struggles with the idea of a man his age with his daughter, but I think he's mostly gotten over it. We're still friends, but we no longer talk babes or typical bro stuff.

Layla closes the door and turns back to me with a mischievous smile. She saunters over to me, her beautiful hips swaying and her belly gently rounded. My throat goes dry at the sight of her.

"Hey, Daddy," she greets me with a sweet smile as

she ropes her arms around my neck. "Is it time for your rub now?"

I nod my head seriously. "You already know it, baby doll. Daddy's aching."

She pouts out her bottom lip and makes bedroom eyes at me. "Where? I'll rub it for you and make it all better."

I grab her hand and place it on my swollen cock. "Right here." I squeeze myself with her hand.

Her eyes darken with lust, and she bites her lip. "You want me to rub you there?"

"Yes, baby. That'll make Daddy feel so good," I croak.

Layla palms me through my pants. I throw my head back and groan at the delicious friction. "Fuck," I murmur when I feel her unzip me. I fall out into her waiting hands, hot and heavy. My balls are full and already churning. It's been too long since this morning.

"Maybe if I kiss it, it'll make it feel better." She blinks up at me.

"Fuck," I grit, chest heaving as I take in strangled breaths. It's always like this. Layla has me on the brink of madness. "Daddy would love that, princess."

Layla falls to her knees and kisses the head of my cock, gently swirling her tongue around the tip, teasing me. I fist my hands into her hair as I hold her head still and thrust gently inside her mouth until I hit the back of her throat. My eyes roll back in my head, and I make myself stop.

She takes over, using both of her hands and her sweet lips to suck and jerk on me at the same time. I moan, a deep guttural sound, "Keep doing that, princess, and you're going to make Daddy come."

"Come?" She looks up at me questioningly.

She's immersed in her role, and I don't hesitate to give her exactly what she needs. I'll be her daddy anytime if that's what my girl wants. "Yeah, it's when you make Daddy feel good and white stuff spurts out of him."

"Out of here?" She licks the slit of my cock, and I nearly come on the spot.

"Yes, baby doll, out of there."

"I want to see it," she says eagerly, pumping me.

"Keep doing that, and you will soon," I growl, my balls drawing up and preparing to shoot their load.

Layla goes back to sucking on the head of my cock while jerking my length. I swell with the onset of my orgasm, but before I can warn her, she pops her lips off me, and I go shooting up into the air. Sticky ropes shoot straight up and fall in an arc onto her pretty face.

She doesn't flinch. Instead, she closes her eyes and basks in my cum while I cover her face with load after load of my sticky essence. The sight is so erotic that my knees shake, and I feel like I'm going to pass out. I lean against the wall, completely spent, and watch in amazement as Layla scoops my cum from her face and licks it from her fingers like a kitten lapping up cream.

"Mmm," she moans. "You taste so good, Daddy. I want more."

My cock is already hard again. Fuck, I'll never get enough of her. "I'm going to give you more, but this time I'm going to put it in your sweet little pussy where it's meant to go so you can make Daddy a baby."

Unable to control myself, I yank her to her feet and slam into her with one hard thrust. She gasps, clinging to me as I rut into her savagely. "You want Daddy to breed you, princess?"

"Yes!" she screams. "Breed me, Daddy! Put a baby up in me!"

Never mind that she's currently pregnant. The thought of breeding her turns us both on to no end, and when we both come together, I know if she weren't already pregnant, she would be now.

It doesn't matter how many kids we have. Layla will always be my princess. Now and forever.

THE END

Welcome to a filthy dirty summer! Drop it like it's hot with your 17 favorite instalove authors! Each stand-alone story delivers a scorching, fantasy-fueled romance! No need to pack a swimsuit—your kindle is all you need for a wet and wild summer! Read the other books in the Filthy Dirty Summer series!

Connect with Emma!

Visit Emma's website to get a FREE book you can't get anywhere else: www.authoremmabray.com.